Please return or renew this item by the last date
shown.

Libraries Line and Renewals: **020 7361 3010**

Web Renewals: www.rbkc.gov.uk/renewyourbooks

KENSINGTON AND CHELSEA LIBRARY SERVICE

First published in Great Britain in 2017 by
Piccadilly Press
80-81 Wimpole Street, London, W1G 9RE
www.piccadillypress.co.uk

This is a work of fiction. Names, places, events and incidents are either the
products of the author's imagination or are used fictitiously. Any resemblance to
actual persons, living or dead, or actual events, is purely coincidental.

A CIP catalogue record for this book is available from the British Library.

ISBN: 978–1–848–12633–6
also available as an ebook

1 3 5 7 9 10 8 6 4 2

Typeset in Berkeley Oldstyle
Printed and bound by Clays Ltd, St Ives PLC

Piccadilly Press is an imprint of Bonnier Zaffre,
a Bonnier Publishing Company
www.bonnierpublishingfiction.co.uk

FLYING FERGUS

The Wreck-it Race

CHRIS HOY
with Joanna Nadin

Illustrations by Clare Elsom

Piccadilly
PRESS

Meet Fergus
and his friends...

Fergus

Chimp

Grandpa Herc

Daisy

Jambo Patterson

Mum

Mikey McLeod

Wesley Wallace

Minnie McLeod

Calamity Coogan

Dermot Eggs

Charlie Campbell

Sorcha

Choppy Wallace

Belinda Bruce

. . .and see where they live

Fergus's house

Daisy's house

NAPIER STREET

Herc's Hand-Me-Downs

Bandstand

Play park

CARNOUSTIE COMMON

Bruce's Biscuits

Meet Princess Lily
and her friends...

Hector Hamilton

Princess Lily

Unlucky Luke

Percy the Pretty Useless

Demelza

Douglas

Dimmock

Queen Woebegot

King Woebegot

Prince Waldorf

Prince Derek

Hounds of Horribleness

Knights of No Nonsense

Scary Mary

THE CASTLE

Turret of Terror

Stables

Entrance to dungeon

Cook's pantry

Hounds of Horribleness Kennels

THE TRAINING TRACK

THE ENCHANTED FOREST

Hercules' Show-offs

Fergus Hamilton was an ordinary nine-year-old boy. He liked his best friend Daisy (even when she was correcting him on bicycle facts). He liked his teammates Calamity and Minnie (especially when Calamity crashed spectacularly or Minnie pulled off an amazing alleyoop). He even liked his former arch-nemesis Wesley Wallace (except when he was showing off, which was still at least once a day).

He didn't much like his Deputy Head, Mr Minto, (because he was always telling Fergus that brains were more important than bicycles).

Or Belinda's dad, Brian Bruce the Biscuit Baron, (because he thought Belinda was better than all the rest of the team put together).

And he absolutely did not like Miss Briggs from number fourteen (because she insisted his dog Chimp had done a poo in her garden, when everyone knows it was Mrs MacCafferty's cat, Carol).

Yes, he was ordinary in almost every way, except one. Because, for a small boy, Fergus Hamilton had an extraordinarily big imagination.

Some days he imagined he was King of the World and would invent laws to ban broccoli and being mean, and give everyone free cake on a Tuesday.

NO BEING MEAN!!
(by order of King Fergus)

FREE CAKE TUESDAY

NO BROCCOLI MORE CAKE!

Some days he imagined he was King of Nevermore, the parallel universe where his dad lived, and would make cycling a national sport, and put his friend Princess Lily in charge of picking teams, instead of her dad, King Woebegot, who barely even believed cycling should exist.

And some days he imagined he was just king of their flat on Napier Street and could stop his mum and her fiancé Jambo talking about weddings all the time, stop Grandpa cutting his toenails on the sofa, and stop Chimp trying to lick the clippings.

But this morning Fergus was imagining the Hercules' Hopefuls standing on the winners' podium at the Internationals, the trophy held high in his own hands amidst the cheers of the adoring crowd, including his hero, Steve "Spokes" Sullivan.

It wasn't even one of his craziest daydreams. His team and Wallace's Winners had made it to the next stage of the competition, and now that they'd got over their squabbling and accepted that they had to race together, they stood a really good chance of taking the prize.

"And here he is, 'Flying' Fergus Hamilton himself, who has single-handedly led his team to this incredible triumph," the commentator yelled in his head, as he skidded to a halt past the finish line at track practice. "And just listen to the crowd go wild . . ."

"I doubt it," said Grandpa with a sigh.

Oops. Fergus gulped. He hadn't realised he was shouting out loud. Still, it was true though, wasn't it?

But the look on Grandpa's face suggested otherwise. "Fergie, I hate to say it, but you're two seconds down on your last lap, and ten down on your time for the Nationals."

Fergus frowned. "The clock's wrong," he said. "It's got to be."

Choppy Wallace held out his own stopwatch. "Two clocks can't be wrong," he said.

Fergus felt his pride plummet and his stomach sink. He'd been so sure he was heading for glory.

"Don't feel too bad, sonny," Grandpa patted him on the shoulder. "It's not just you. Everyone's down."

"I don't know what's got into them," Choppy despaired, staring at the rest of the team still dawdling round the track.

"Too big for their boots, that's what," said Grandpa. "I've seen it before. They win one race and think everything is in the bag, a done deal."

"It should be," insisted Choppy, "with my boy in the line-up."

"Well, it's not," said Grandpa. "And if they carry on like this, they're going to find out the hard way, including Wesley."

Choppy's face reddened. "I'll not have my Wesley brought down by . . . lazybones and – and show-offs!"

Ha! Fergus said (but definitely to himself this time), *Wesley's the biggest show-off of all.* As if to prove it, Wesley chose that very moment to fly across the finish line waving both hands in the air, then promptly lost his balance and crashed into Calamity, who smashed into Daisy, who fell on top of Minnie and Mikey, who toppled onto Dermot, who was eating a biscuit and got a piece of pink wafer stuck in his throat and had to have his back smacked by Belinda, who was used to biscuit-based injuries.

"It's not just them," said Grandpa, shaking his head. "It's us too. The coaching's got to change."

Choppy's already scarlet face darkened. "Change? Oh, I see what you're up to. You want to get rid of me, eh?" "Och, no," insisted Grandpa.

But Choppy was too angry to listen. "Well, if you don't like my methods, maybe *you* should quit!" he exploded.

Fergus flinched. He'd thought the two coaches had settled their differences in the highlands, too. But clearly old rivalries died hard.

Grandpa held steady, though. "No one's quitting. In fact, the opposite. I think we need someone else to get them back on track. Some fresh ideas, maybe. A deputy coach, if you like."

"I thought *you* were the deputy," said Choppy, puffing himself up.

"But – but –" spluttered Daisy. Fergus

felt words bursting out of his mouth too – that Grandpa wasn't deputy, he was the best, and should be head coach – but Grandpa raised an eyebrow in warning to the pair of them.

"Leave it to me," was all he said, turning back to Choppy. "I'll come up with someone."

But by teatime the best Grandpa had managed was his old racing buddy Chick Gordon, only he'd moved to Aberdeen, and Kenny Hegarty who'd once coached the Falkirk Flyers, only he'd moved to Australia.

"What about Malky McGovern from the council?" asked Jambo. "He likes a bike ride of a Sunday, and he's a big supporter of the squad."

Grandpa laughed. "A slow spin around Carnoustie Common's not quite what I had in mind. Besides, I know Malky was a big help with the cinder track, but I'm not sure he'd be much of a coach."

"Or you could try Fergie's deputy head," suggested Jambo, as he served up the sausages. "He'll know a thing or two about keeping kids in line."

"Mr Minto?" yelped Fergus, shooing away Chimp, who was desperately trying to snaffle a sausage. "He hates bicycles. And me."

"Now that's not totally true," Mum said, as she lifted her plate so Jambo could spoon another dollop of mash on. "But he is a stickler, and I'm not sure he'd get on with Choppy."

"So who?" asked Fergus, exasperated.

"I've an idea," said Mum, squeezing sauce onto her sausages in one practised move.

Grandpa looked up. "Who?" he asked.

"Yes, who?" echoed Jambo. "We're all ears."

But Mum just looked mysterious as she speared her sausage with a fork. "You'll see," she said. "Just leave it to me."

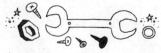

Fergus lay in bed that night wondering what, exactly, Mum was up to. She knew a lot of things, especially about being a nurse – how to fix broken arms, and what your heart rate should be, and which bacteria were good ones and which were bad – but as far as he was aware, she wasn't a world expert on bikes, and besides, she didn't know any cyclists except for him and the team. Unless . . .

He turned to Chimp, who was chewing a shoe. "Do you think Mum might be a long lost friend of Spokes Sullivan?" he said hopefully.

Chimp, who was still feeling hard done by over the lack of sausages, let go of the shoe, then dropped his head down on his paws with a harumphing sigh.

At that, Fergus's hopes dropped too. "My thoughts exactly," he said. "And besides, we don't even need a new coach. We're absolutely fine just as we are."

But as he pulled the duvet tight, and remembered the arguments, and how slow they were all going, he wondered if that was really true.

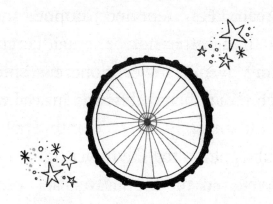

A Chance for Charlie

"I reckon it's Betty Burton," said Daisy, sucking on a liquorice stick as the gang sat trackside, waiting for the grown-ups to show.

"A woman?" demanded Wesley. "Don't be daft."

"Who's being daft?" said Fergus indignantly. "She's won more races than you've had hot dinners."

"I doubt it," said Wesley. "Anyway, it's more likely to be Legs McPhee."

"Yeah, Legs," repeated Dermot.

"It had better not be," said Fergus, feeling a cold shiver along his spine as he remembered the awful way Legs had deliberately swerved into Spokes to take gold at the Olympics.

"Well, we're about to find out," said Mikey, nodding his head towards Grandpa and Choppy who were hurrying across the track, followed by someone else. Someone who didn't look like Spokes Sullivan, or any cycle coaches Fergus had ever heard of.

"Who's that?" hissed Minnie.

"Well, it's not Legs McPhee, that's for sure," said Wesley. "Unless he's taken to using a wheelchair."

"Legs McPhee's a man," pointed out Calamity. "And *she* most certainly isn't."

Fergus looked hard at the woman wheeling towards them, with "Girls

Rule" emblazoned on her sweatshirt.

"Well she's got that right," said Daisy, grinning. "So she's not Betty Burton, but she's still a *she*. Though I have no idea who."

Fergus shook his head. "Nor me," he admitted. "Mum wouldn't tell me anything at breakfast – just said it would be a surprise."

"Well it's *that* all right," said Wesley. "Though not the good kind. I bet she's never ridden a bike in her life."

"You don't know anything about her," whispered Daisy. "Give her a chance."

"Give who a chance?" said the woman, pulling up in front of them. "Me?"

Fergus could feel his face redden. Even though he hadn't said anything bad, he'd not told Wesley to shut up either.

"It's all right," said the woman, her stern face dissolving into a wide smile. "Nothing I'm not used to. Now, I suppose you're wondering who I am."

Fergus and the others nodded silently.

"My name's Charlotte Campbell," she said. "But my friends – and enemies – call me Charlie."

Charlie Campbell . . . Fergus did recognise that name, and from the telly too. But not from bikes, from . . .

"Basketball!" he blurted. "You were on the women's team in the Paralympics!"

"Not just *on* it," Grandpa pointed out. "Charlie *captained* it."

"So why aren't you coaching *them*?" asked Wesley, bitterly.

"Oh, I am," said Charlie, laughing. "Which is why we've already qualified for next year's Worlds. But our season doesn't start for a couple of months, so when my favourite nurse Jeanie said her son's cycling squad needed a bit of tough love, I said I'd give it a go."

Tough love, Fergus thought to himself. That didn't sound great. And there was something else bothering him too. And clearly bothering the others.

"I don't mean to be rude," Daisy began, "but bikes and basketball aren't really the same thing."

"That's what I said," agreed Choppy, glaring at Grandpa. "Not the same thing at all."

"That's okay," Charlie replied, smiling again at Daisy. "If I were you, I'd be asking questions too, but, like I pointed out to the *lovely* Choppy here, fitness and focus are the same whatever sport you're playing."

Lovely Choppy! Fergus grinned. He could feel himself warming to this woman. And yes, bikes and basketballs were different, but she was right, all teams needed to band together, to push themselves and each other, and to focus on the final goal. And they'd not been managing much of that lately, despite their newfound friendship in the mountains. So maybe, just maybe, Charlie could be the golden ticket to glory after all. With that seed of hope glowing inside him, Fergus picked up his bike and wheeled it straight to the start line. He was ready for whatever Charlie threw at them, even if that was tough love.

Absolute Beginners

"Yoga?" yelled Wesley. "You have *got* to be joking!"

"Yoga?" spluttered Calamity. "With *my* legs? I don't think so."

"Yoga?" Fergus repeated. That wasn't what he'd had in mind when he'd said to himself he was ready for anything. He must have heard it wrong, surely.

"No, you didn't hear me wrong," Charlie said, as if she could see straight into Fergus's head, making his cheeks flush pink again. "Bikes are banned for now, it's your brains and bodies we're going to concentrate on. So come back inside, the lot of you. No dilly-dallying, we've got the Internationals to win."

The squad turned to Choppy and Grandpa, waiting for one of them to say something – anything. Surely Choppy would put a stop to this? Get them back on their bikes at least? But for once Choppy was lost for words, and all Grandpa could say was, "You heard the lady, off you go."

"'Coach', if you don't mind," Charlie corrected.

"Aye, you're right," agreed Grandpa grinning. "Coach Campbell it is."

Confused, but still determined to give Charlie a chance, Fergus locked his bike in the store along with the others, and then led the squad towards the changing rooms: Belinda and Daisy dejected, Minnie and Mikey muttering to each other, and Calamity concentrating on not tripping over Dermot and Wesley, who were pushing each other into the walls as they went. The only one who seemed happy with the arrangement was Chimp, who sat snug on Charlie's lap, cadging a lift.

"At least it'll be easy," Minnie whispered as they laid out their mats and sat cross-legged, just as Charlie had told them to.

"Easy peasy," Mikey agreed.

"We'll probably fall asleep," Wesley scoffed.

"Shhhh," whispered Fergus, although he quietly wondered if they might be right. Just how hard could yoga be?

"Owwww," Fergus found himself complaining five minutes later as he tried to bend his legs into the lotus position.

"Double owwww!" wailed Wesley who was stuck in a downward dog.

"Ooops," cried Calamity as he toppled over from his tree pose straight on top of Dermot, who was still struggling to work out which leg was his left one.

Charlie tried hard to stifle a giggle. "Not so easy peasy now, is it?" she said.

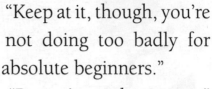

"Keep at it, though, you're not doing too badly for absolute beginners."

"But we're not beginners," said Wesley, as Choppy helped haul him into an upright position. "We're champions."

"Champions," agreed Dermot, who had given up on guessing which leg was which and was focusing on not being flattened again.

"You *were* champions," corrected Charlie. "And I'm not knocking that; winning the Nationals was an amazing achievement, and you *should* be proud. But pride comes before a fall. And we want to avoid that, don't we?"

"I s'pose," admitted Wesley.

"And I've done enough of that already," sighed Calamity.

"Definitely," Fergus said, winning himself a wink from Grandpa.

"Good," said Charlie. "So you want to be going into your next race not sitting on your laurels but chasing your dream, hungry for it."

"And yoga's supposed to teach them that?" demanded Choppy.

"Yoga gives them focus," said Charlie. "And it helps to build strength and stamina too."

"And flexibility," added Grandpa, joining in. "Come on, Choppy, give it a go!"

"Oh, very well, if I must." Choppy bent over to touch his toes.

"Oh," he said in surprise as he found himself unable to get further than halfway.

"Keep stretching," Charlie told him. "All of you. You're never going to get it first time. Stop looking at what *others* are doing and focus on what *you* can achieve."

Fergus remembered what Grandpa always used to say to him: "Just when you think you've got nothing left, dig deep for a final push." *Go on*, he told himself, *you can do it*. And focusing as hard as he could he pulled his legs until they rested on top of each other, feeling muscles he didn't even know he had getting a workout for the first time. And feeling more than a little satisfaction, too.

"See?" said Charlie, who had wheeled next to him. "Good, isn't it, getting out of your comfort zone?"

"Aye." Fergus nodded.

"Yes, yes," said Choppy, standing up swiftly. "This is all very well, but the squad needs to be racing; they need to find their fighting spirit."

"And they will," assured Charlie. "They will."

"But when?" whined Wesley. "I want my bike back!"

"Just as soon as you can all do a tree for a minute without falling over." Charlie winked.

Wesley rolled his eyes. "I'll be back on the track in ten minutes then."

"Tomorrow more like." Daisy laughed.

"This time, next week," Fergus trumped her, though he couldn't keep the air of gloom out of his voice. After all, what was the point of training for a bike race without a bike?

Fergus wasn't far wrong. It was four days before they found out just what Charlie had in store – four days in which they'd learned to sit for five minutes in the lotus position, practised push-ups until they could do twenty without pausing, and whizzed round in wheelbarrows without dropping each other once.

"I think you're ready now," Charlie announced, as Calamity managed to cross the room without tripping over his own feet or getting tangled in Minnie's.

"Ready for what?" Fergus asked

eagerly. He'd actually quite enjoyed all the yoga, not that he let on to Wesley, but he was itching to get in the saddle again; to feel the wind in his face as he pedalled for all he was worth – to feel like he was flying.

"For this!" Charlie announced, as Grandpa unfurled an enormous poster.

"The Wreck-it Run," read Fergus out loud. "Are you serious?"

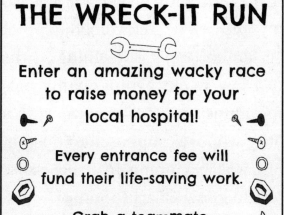

THE WRECK-IT RUN

Enter an amazing wacky race
to raise money for your
local hospital!

Every entrance fee will
fund their life-saving work.

Grab a teammate,
design your winning entry
and come along . . .

"The what-now?" asked Belinda.

Wesley pulled a face. "Is that even a race?"

"Aye," Fergus said. "It's a race, all right. But not with bikes." He felt his tummy flip as he remembered Mum telling Jambo to put something in the paper a few weeks ago: a charity race to raise money for the hospital, with a celebrity who was supposed to open it. Now it was beginning to make sense how Mum knew Charlie. Sort of.

"With what then?" demanded Daisy.

Fergus looked at Charlie, who nodded

at him to go ahead. "With . . . with machines," he managed finally. "With home-made machines."

The squad was silent for a moment as they took that in.

"But . . ." began Belinda, "what sort of machines are we talking about?"

"That's the best bit," said Charlie enthusiastically. "You can build anything you want."

"Oooh. Like my dad's motorised golf cart?" suggested Belinda, eyes wide in excitement.

"Not exactly." Charlie smiled. "No motors. That's the beauty of it. Plus you do it in pairs – one sitting in the vehicle steering, one pushing – and, best of all, it has to be built from everyday objects."

"Like recycling?" asked Calamity.

"Exactly," said Grandpa. "Make do

and mend, you know my motto."

"I don't see why we can't just cycle," muttered Choppy. "Or buy go-karts. At least then we'd know we were going to win."

"Because," said Charlie, "that's not the point. The point is that it's something everyone has a real chance of winning. The point is to raise money for the hospital. The point is –"

"To take us out of our comfort zones," Fergus interrupted.

"Bingo," Charlie said. "It's time to think outside the box."

Machine Madness

The squad assembled in the yard at the back of Grandpa's shop, Hercules' Hand-Me-Downs. Here were wooden pallets, old wheels, and odd bits of scrap from who knows what.

Choppy looked round with a sneer. "Scrap metal and junk," he said. "Is that what we've come to?"

Wesley turned up his nose, too.

"What's the matter?" asked Daisy. "Worried about rust on your new top?"

"Or a spider wriggling up your sleeve?" questioned Calamity.

Fergus smiled: his lot loved this place – they were always in here fine-tuning and fixing their bikes – but Wesley was used to Wallace's Wheels with its brand-new Sullivan Swifts and box-fresh bike parts.

"Och, there'll be a spider or two, and you'll probably want to pop on an old top," Grandpa said. "But there's nothing to worry about."

"Nothing to worry about?" blustered Wesley. "We've got to build things from this junk! With our – our bare hands!"

"Isn't it exciting?" Charlie smiled. "Right, first things first: you'll need to team up in pairs."

Fergus looked at Daisy quickly. The Wreck-it Run was going to be a massive challenge, but at the very least he wanted his best friend by his side, that was for sure.

Daisy grinned back. "Team?" she said.

"Team!" he agreed, then, relieved, glanced round the room to see Wesley paired up with Dermot, Belinda with Minnie, and Calamity with Mikey.

"Grand," said Charlie. "That means Herc and Choppy, you get to go together."

"Me?" demanded Choppy. "You've got to be joking."

"Us?" asked Grandpa. "Och, I'm not sure."

"Listen to the pair of you!," said Charlie. "There'll be all ages and all abilities entering. Herc, if you're worried about having enough power to push, Choppy can do that and you can steer."

Grandpa thought for a moment.

"Go on," Fergus encouraged him. He knew that however much Grandpa loved to coach, he missed the buzz of racing since his knees had started giving him trouble. But he could steer – he could steer for Scotland!

"Yeah, go on, Dad," agreed Wesley for once. "You're always moaning about how you could do everything better. Now's your chance."

"Aye, maybe we should," Grandpa said, turning to Choppy with a grin and a glint in his eye. "What do you say? With you as the power, me as the steering. I may be an ageing tiger, but I'm still a tiger after all."

"I– I –" stammered Choppy.

"Grand!" exclaimed Charlie. "That's settled then. Next job: design your machine."

"How do we do that?" asked Minnie.

"Take a look around," said Charlie, "and grab whatever takes your fancy. Just bear in mind it needs to be sturdy and stable and speedy."

"And no motors," added Daisy, one eye always on the rules.

"Herc, you can help with the building bit, can't you?" said Charlie, seeing the concern on the squad's faces – Wesley's in particular.

"Of course," Grandpa confirmed. "But the design is down to you lot. So get your thinking caps on."

Fergus and Daisy gazed around them, taking in the bits and bobs and odds and ends.

"I like the look of those," said Daisy, nodding at a set of old pram wheels with proper treaded tyres.

"Nice," said Fergus, reaching up to pull them off the shelf. "Oh. There's only three, though."

"So?" said Daisy. "We have one in front and two at the back."

"Like a trike?" asked Fergus.

"Exactly," said Daisy. "It'll be beast! Nice and light, but easy to steer and stable too."

"Brilliotic!" Fergus agreed. Charlie's ideas may be off the wall but they were also way more fun than he'd thought . . . almost worth having his bike in lock-down for. "How about this for the body?" he asked, pointing at a red plastic sledge. "There's room for one of us on board – and even Chimp too!"

"I'm not sure he'll be interested," said Daisy.

Fergus looked over at Chimp and frowned. His faithful friend had barely left Charlie's lap all week except to come home for tea, and even then he'd whined.

"Och, he'll get bored when she runs out of dog biscuits," Daisy said, seeing Fergus's face fall. "Come on, we've got tonnes of work to do."

"Suppose," Fergus said. "You're probably right."

"Probably?" Daisy said with a smile. "I'm ALWAYS right. At least most of the time."

Fergus smiled back. Yes, whatever Chimp was up to, and Charlie, this Wreck-it Run was at least going to be fun.

It took two days, three changes of design and several splinters, but, by Sunday afternoon, Daisy and Fergus – as well as the rest of the squad – had built their magnificent machines.

Wesley and Dermot's was made from old car panels, and spray-painted jet black with a flame design down the side. "She's called *The Invincible*," announced Wesley.

"Is that so?" asked Charlie. "Well, let's take your word for it."

Minnie and Belinda's was long and low, with a glass visor for wind protection. "It's from a washing machine," Minnie said proudly, and Charlie nodded in approval.

"Nice," said Grandpa. "We've got washing machine bearings too, and a bit of a lawnmower!"

"Washing machines, lawnmowers," grumbled Choppy. "I never thought I'd see the day."

"Ours is a bit . . . rickety," admitted Calamity as he and Mikey stood back to let Charlie inspect their work.

"Maybe so," agreed Charlie, "but you've got pedal power as well as someone pushing, so as long as it lasts the race, you're in with a brilliant chance."

Pedals! Fergus cursed himself for not thinking of that – he was a cyclist after all. Now what hope did he and Daisy have on an old sledge, even with the greased axles and steering wheel Grandpa had helped them attach?

He felt his heart sink as Charlie came to check it over.

But Charlie seemed to think differently. "Not bad," she said, giving it the once over. "Not bad at all."

"Really?" asked Fergus. "You're not just saying that?"

"I never lie," said Charlie. "No point telling someone they're better than they are or have more chance than they do. That's the road to disappointment."

"But we've not got pedals," said Fergus. "Or car panels. And it's not as sleek as Minnie and Belinda's either."

"But we've got great steering," said Daisy, pulling a face at Fergus.

"You have," said Charlie. "And it's sturdy too. So stop worrying about what others have got, and focus on your own plus points. Play to your strengths!"

Fergus felt guilt whoosh through him like a bucket of cold water on embers as he remembered Spokes's motto: "Believe in yourself, and others will follow."

"We will," he promised quickly. "Won't we, Daisy?"

"I always do," Daisy said with a wink. "So when can we test run them?"

"No time like the present," Charlie replied. "What do you say, gang?"

"Let's do it!" Fergus whooped. He was fired up and ready to rumble. So he and Daisy might not have the best bearings or extra pedals, but they'd worked hard on their machine, and with Daisy's precision steering and his leg power, they were in with a shot.

Weren't they?

Nervous Wrecks

"Quit pushing," whined Wesley, as the teams jostled on the start line. "You'll snap our wing mirror!"

"There's no room," complained Calamity, untangling his foot from one of Belinda's spokes.

"Stop moaning, the lot of you!" ordered Charlie. "You can't expect this to be easy. This is a Wreck-it Run, things are going to get . . . a little messy. So, safety checks, please."

Fergus made sure his helmet was fastened and his knee-pads were tight. Better safe than sorry, as Daisy's mum was fond of saying, and right now, looking at the crazy contraptions lining up alongside him, he couldn't agree more. As it was, Mrs Devlin had only agreed to let Daisy race because the Wreck-it Run was being held in the grounds of the hospital, so emergency help was at hand.

"Okay, on your marks . . ." Charlie cried, "Get set . . . GO!"

Fergus pushed with all his might and felt the machine lurch forward so hard he almost plunged to the floor. It was lighter than he'd imagined, but less precise, too, even with Daisy's expert steering. But as his feet pounded the tarmac, he felt himself fall into a rhythm and felt Daisy get to grips with the turns, and soon they were taking the corners without swerving off course, or slamming into the others.

Sadly, the same couldn't be said of everyone. Before they'd even made it down the back straight, Calamity and Mikey had hit the side barriers, Minnie and Belinda had spun a doughnut and careered onto the grass and as for Wesley and Dermot, they were still arguing over which was the brake and which was the horn.

Then, as Fergus and Daisy turned onto the final straight, they found themselves face to face with Grandpa and Choppy who were struggling with steering and had managed to do half the lap backwards instead.

"Slow down!" yelled Daisy.

"I'm trying!" cried Fergus.

But try as he might, he couldn't pull up in time and instead the pair slammed into the other machine with a sickening *CRUNCH!*

"I'm so sorry," Fergus apologised, feeling tears well in his eyes at the thought of hurting Grandpa or Daisy or even Choppy.

"Hey, hey," Grandpa comforted. "No harm done. Well, nothing that can't be fixed with glue or nails, anyway."

Fergus surveyed the damage – Grandpa was right, it was just dents, and a wobbly wheel or two.

"And it is a Wreck-it Run," Charlie pointed out. "Crashing is half the fun."

"Exactly," said Daisy, climbing out happily. "That was BEAST!"

"It's BANANAS," insisted Wesley, crossly. "How has this got anything to do with Internationals?"

"Yeah, how?" demanded Dermot.

"I don't even think I know which way is forward anymore," muttered Minnie, as she staggered dizzily around.

"Resilience," said Charlie. "That's what this is teaching you. Flexibility, too. And maybe even . . . fun?"

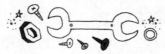

But back in the changing rooms, fun was the last thing on anyone's mind.

"We need to take a stand," insisted Wesley. "Show them who's in charge."

"Charlie's in charge," said Daisy. "And I like her."

"That's just because she said you had decent steering," Wesley sneered.

"No it's not," Daisy snapped back. "She's got loads of good ideas. And Fergus agrees with me. Don't you, Fergus?"

Fergus pretended he hadn't heard. He liked Charlie a lot, but Wesley had a point: even if it was only the machines that got bruised and battered, how did that help them win the Internationals? And she'd not even been letting them near their bikes – she said she had reasons but he couldn't work out what on earth they were.

"We should go on strike," suggested Mikey.

"Until what?" asked Minnie.

"Until we get a better coach," said Wesley.

"But who?" barked Belinda. "Charlie was the only person anyone could come up with."

An idea flashed into Fergus's head, bright as a lightbulb. There was someone – someone he knew cared about the squad, someone who knew about bikes, someone who'd won cycling championships himself.

His dad, Hector Hamilton.

Fergus would have to persuade him to come back from Nevermore, but it couldn't be harder than anything Charlie had got them to do.

Could it?

"Where are you off to?" asked Daisy, as Fergus sidled towards the door.

"Nowhere," he said quickly. "Well, I just need to pop out. There's . . . something I need to do."

"Now?" Daisy said. "Really?"

Fergus shrugged. "See you back here tomorrow?"

Daisy shook her head. "Bonkers," she said. "Okay, tomorrow it is."

Fergus took a deep breath. Maybe he *was* bonkers. But if it could sort the team spirit out, it was worth a try.

Holding on to that thought, he slipped out the door to bust his bike out of lockdown.

Grandpa kept the key to the store in the pocket of his jacket, which hung on the back of office door. Getting the key had been the easy part, as the coaches were all still trackside. But persuading Chimp to come with him was proving much, much harder. All his dog wanted to do these days was sit on Charlie's lap. Or so it seemed.

"Come on, boy," Fergus called for the third time..

Chimp finally cocked an ear and opened an eye, but thought better of whatever it was and went back to having his tummy tickled as Charlie and Grandpa talked tactics.

"Chimp," Fergus tried again, more loudly.

But the dog was having none of it.

"Fine," he said. "Guess I'm on my own then." And he left him there while he headed to the bike store.

As he unlocked the store door and then his bike, he felt his heart hammering. He wasn't supposed to ride at all. This was going against Charlie – and Grandpa. And, what if he couldn't get to Nevermore without Chimp anyway? What if it wasn't just backpedalling that did it – what if Chimp was the secret ingredient?

But he had no choice, Fergus told himself. The squad needed him, and he'd do anything to help them. So slick as a snake and quiet as a mouse he wheeled his bike out to the car park.

Sitting in the saddle, he tightened his helmet, and took a deep breath. "I can do this," he said aloud. "I have to do this."

"Woof!" agreed a voice.

Fergus turned and felt the butterflies in his tummy flit away at the sight of his faithful friend. "Oh so you *are* speaking to me, are you?" he said. "Well, I hope your legs can keep up after all that sitting around, we've got work to do."

Because to get to Nevermore Fergus would have to ride as hard as he could for the magic to happen. And right now he really needed that magic.

His legs were a little rusty, but soon they were speeding across the concrete. Fergus tucked his head down and elbows in without even thinking – aerodynamics were as natural to him now as breathing. A little more effort and he could feel they'd hit the sweet spot. He closed his eyes and let his feet backpedal – once, twice, three times . . .

Team Trial Trauma

"Waaahhhh!" he yelled as he found himself whizzing through Queen Woebegot's prize petunias in the palace garden before coming to a crash in the compost.

"Interesting landing," said a voice.

"Lily!" he replied, as his friend helped haul him to his feet. "Sorry about the flowers," he said, looking back at the path of devastation he'd cut through the middle of the bed.

"Oh, we'll sort those out later," said Lily. "Bit rusty, are we?"

"Rusty? I should coco," grumbled another voice, this one from under the compost.

Fergus and Lily pushed a pile of potato peelings aside to find Chimp with an eggshell wedged on each ear.

Lily laughed as she plucked them off. "Well, I'm just glad you two made it at all. You're just in time, come on!"

"In time for what?" Chimp asked, as he and Fergus hopped back on the bike and hurried after Lily.

"Beats me," said Fergus, but whatever it was, his dad was sure to be involved, and at that thought, he picked up the pace, feeling again the thrill of being back on a bike.

"What in the name of Waltzing Matilda needed that kind of speed?" asked Chimp, as they came to a halt at Nevermore's brand new and unusual cycle track, where Unlucky Luke, Prince Waldorf, and his sidekick, Dimmock, were waiting.

"Team trials," said Unlucky Luke, gloomily. "All right, Fergus?"

Fergus nodded back a greeting. "But I thought you'd all just be on the team, you two and Waldorf and Dimwit – I mean, Dimmock." Fergus smiled. He knew he should have felt bad about getting Waldorf's sidekick's name wrong, but the boy really was a bit of a fool.

"Dimwit or not, he should still be on the team," barked Waldorf. "As should I."

"And me," Luke said miserably.

"Well, in your case I can understand it," scorned Waldorf. "Until you get those chicken feet fixed you're no use on legs, let alone wheels. But me? I'm the fastest cyclist in the Kingdom."

"Well, we don't actually know that yet," Lily pointed out to her brother. "Which is why Hector wanted to hold the trials. What if there's someone super speedy living in a far-flung corner of Nevermore?"

At the mention of his dad's name, Fergus felt his spirits lift immediately. His dad really did know best about bikes. Better than Charlie, he was sure of it. Not that Waldorf thought so.

"I doubt it," the prince scoffed. "Have you looked at that lot? Not one of them seems to know how to ride."

Fergus gazed at the gathering crowd. Waldorf had a point: there were a lot of people lining up to take their turn on the trial bikes, but most were falling off, or getting on backwards . . .

"Hardly surprising," said Lily, "seeing as cycling was banned until a few months ago."

"So why bother with trials?" Fergus asked out loud.

"Just in case," came the reply. Hector Hamilton was walking towards Fergus with a smile on his face.

"Dad!" Fergus cried, and hugged his father.

"All right, all right," Chimp muttered. "Back to business. In case of what?"

Fergus let go of his dad and looked at him expectantly.

"In case there's a cycling natural out there. Winning races is about hard work, but talent helps too, and one of these kids just might have what it takes. It's only fair to offer everybody an equal opportunity. Everyone has to start somewhere."

Waldorf made a snorting sound.

"I seem to recall you practically running me over when you first started," Fergus's dad warned the prince.

"But you – you weren't even here then . . ." Waldorf scratched his head.

"Cat," Dimmock said.

"Huh?" said Fergus.

"Where?" demanded Chimp, warily.

"Him," Dimmock said, pointing at Hector. "He was a cat, wasn't he?"

Fergus remembered – of course,

Unlucky Luke's dad had turned his dad into the kitchen cat, Suet. Maybe Dimmock wasn't such a fool after all.

"Right, now we've dredged up that depressing memory, shall we get to work?" Dad suggested.

Everyone nodded.

"Good," he replied. "Then let's get cracking."

"Dad?" Fergus asked as they headed for the start line. "I need to ask you something."

"And you can, but not until this is sorted. Here." He handed Fergus his clipboard with the competitor list.

"What's this for?" Fergus asked.

"I can't do everything, can I?" Dad replied. "You're my assistant coach. I'll need your help."

Fergus nodded. He'd forgotten how much work Dad had cut out for him here: setting up the track, and organising races, as well as taking on coaching the team. Nevermore needed Hector, that was for sure. But Fergus needed him more. Then it pinged into Fergus's head – if he helped Dad out now, then Dad would have to help *him* in return. That's definitely how it worked.

Or at least, that was what Fergus told himself as he got into place, ready for the first contestant.

The Palace Pedallers

"This is hopeless," Lily sighed, after the tenth rider had fallen off in front of the starting line.

"Ridiculous, more like," Waldorf said.

"Dad?" Fergus said, gently.

"Okay, okay," Dad replied. "I admit, it's not looking great."

That was an understatement, Fergus thought to himself. So far, apart from Lily and Waldorf, who were certs anyway, only two people had even made it round the course: Unlucky Luke, who had lived up to his name and got his claws tangled in the pedals, coming a cropper a few times and falling over the finish line, and Mary the kitchen maid, otherwise known as "Scary", on account of her mother being the terrifying Cook. Mary didn't seem to be trying to live up to her nickname: when Dad told her she'd made the team she hadn't said a word, just gone bright red.

And to cap it all, Dimmock had spent most of his round trying to run into other contestants, earning himself a three-month ban from King Woebegot in the process.

"There's only one person left to try out," Lily sighed.

"Then let's hope he's a bobby dazzler," said Dad.

Fergus took a deep breath. The thin, pale boy with his dark sunglasses and large helmet didn't look up to much, but then, he supposed, nor had he with his second-hand bike. Or the rest of Hercules' Hopefuls come to it, like Calamity with his crashing, or Minnie, who was smaller than some of the under-7s. Looks could be deceiving, he knew that for sure.

"Ready?" Fergus called out to the boy.

The boy nodded, and lowered his head.

A good sign already, Fergus thought. "On your marks, get set, GO!" he yelled.

And with that, the good sign turned into a *great* one. The boy was unbelievably speedy, spinning down the straights and cornering with ease.

"Woah!" Chimp exclaimed.

"My thoughts exactly," said Waldorf. "What's his name?"

Fergus checked the clipboard. "It just says 'P-D'."

"Well, whatever his name is, I reckon he's made the team as first rider," said Dad, as the mystery boy crossed the finish with two seconds on Lily and three on Waldorf.

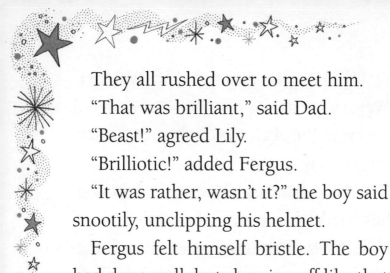

They all rushed over to meet him.

"That was brilliant," said Dad.

"Beast!" agreed Lily.

"Brilliotic!" added Fergus.

"It was rather, wasn't it?" the boy said snootily, unclipping his helmet.

Fergus felt himself bristle. The boy had done well, but showing off like that was bad form.

"So, PD?" said Chimp, before Fergus could blurt anything. "What's that stand for, then?"

The boy pulled off his helmet, took off his sunglasses and looked with disdain at the group assembled before him. "Derek," he replied. "*Prince* Derek to you."

Fergus frowned. Lily and Waldorf didn't have a brother, did they?

"W-what?" stammered Waldorf. "Cousin Derek? Derek . . . Dastardly?"

"Son of Duke Dastardly, ruler of the Darklands, and Dad's biggest rival?" spluttered Lily.

"The very same," gloated Prince Derek. He flicked his long, blonde fringe out of his face. "My dad is rather a devil, isn't he?"

"He is to us," said Lily. "Last Christmas he sent me an exploding toy bear."

"And he sent me a fake dog poo," snapped Waldorf. "Only it turned out not to be fake."

"Ugh!" exclaimed Fergus.

"Don't look at me," said Chimp.

"Ha!" laughed Prince Derek. "So he did. What larks!"

"Hardly," said Waldorf. "It took weeks

to wash the smell out of the carpet, and my velvet slippers."

Fergus caught Lily trying not to snigger.

"Well, you probably deserved it," Prince Derek countered quickly.

"I don't understand," said Dad. "If you dislike Nevermore so much, why do you want to be on our team?"

"Your team?" said Prince Derek. "Oh, no, I don't want to be on *your* poxy team. I just wanted to show you what you'll be up against in the first race."

"No way!" cried Lily.

"Yes way," replied Prince Derek. "And mission accomplished, I'd say." With that, he gave his fringe another flick, popped on his helmet, and disappeared off towards the palace drive, where a black hover van was waiting.

"What a dag," said Chimp.

"Good riddance to bad rubbish," snorted Lily.

"Absolutely," said Waldorf, agreeing with his sister for once.

"But that still leaves us one team member short," Dad sighed. "Unless . . ." He turned to Fergus, a strange smile on his face.

"Unless what?" Fergus asked, baffled.

"Unless *you* sign up," his dad replied.

"What?" Fergus blurted. "But I'm the assistant coach. And I don't live in Nevermore. It'd be against the rules."

"So move here," said Lily.

Fergus felt his tummy jump. It wasn't that he hadn't thought about it. But not yet, not now. He was supposed to focusing on getting his dad back to Scotland, not staying here himself. And then there was Mum and the wedding, and all his friends – even Wesley.

"No," he said eventually. "I can't be on the team. But I know someone who should be."

"Who?" asked Lily.

"Yes, do tell," said Waldorf. "Because as far as I can see, the only other possible is Unlucky Luke. And that's, well, impossible."

"He's not wrong," admitted Unlucky Luke. "You saw what happened. My paws can't grip the handlebars and my claws get snagged in the pedals. We'd come last anyway."

"That's what *you* think," said Fergus. "Come on, Luke – and you too, Chimp. We've got some work to do."

"Really?" asked Unlucky Luke.

"Really?" asked Chimp.

"Really," replied Fergus.

It wasn't going to be easy – definitely out of his comfort zone. But with a little help from his friends he reckoned he could pull it off.

"I don't believe it!" said Waldorf as Luke rode round the track for a second time, not as speedy as Lily, or Waldorf, or even Scary Mary, but fast enough, and straight and, more importantly, determined.

"I told you," Fergus grinned.

"A specially adapted bike!" Dad shook his head in amazement. "Now, why didn't I come up with that?"

Fergus shrugged. "Just thinking outside the box," he said, remembering Charlie. Maybe she did know what she was talking about. Well, a little bit anyway.

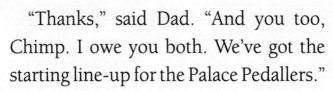

"Thanks," said Dad. "And you too, Chimp. I owe you both. We've got the starting line-up for the Palace Pedallers."

"I love it!" cried Lily.

"Me too," admitted Waldorf.

"Me three." Unlucky Luke grinned, wiggling his chicken feet in their special braces.

Scary Mary just smiled and nodded.

Fergus smiled back. "Well, I reckon it's time to be getting off," he said, turning to Chimp, whose fur was still puffed in pride.

"Er, didn't you want to ask your dad something," his dog said behind his paw.

"I heard that," said Dad. "He's right, you came with a question, Fergus. What was it?"

Fergus took a deep breath. "Nothing," he said. "It doesn't matter."

"Really?" Dad asked.

"Really?" asked Chimp.

"Really," Fergus replied. "Why does no one believe me today?"

"Och, I've always believed in you, son," Dad told him. "You'll be back for the first race, though?"

"I wouldn't miss it for the world!" Fergus smiled. "What, watching you lot beat Prince Derek and his lot?"

"Fingers crossed," said Lily.

"You can do it," said Fergus. "If you practice."

"Aye," agreed Dad. "Good advice from the assistant coach, there. Now, go on then – see you next time, Fergus."

Fergus smiled and clipped on his helmet as Chimp jumped up. "See you," he said. And with that, he pushed his foot down hard on his pedal and set off down the drive.

He should have got it before, he thought as he picked up speed: why Charlie had made them do all the yoga and wheelbarrowing and building the machines for the Wreck-it Run. And why she'd banned the bikes too: because now he was truly hungry for it, now he couldn't wait to get his legs pumping like pistons, to hear the wind whistle past his ears, to feel like he was almost, almost . . . flying!

The Wreck-it Run

"I don't understand," said Daisy, as they wheeled their machine down to the start line in the hospital grounds. "I thought you were on Wesley's side with the others. I thought you wanted Charlie gone?"

"I was," admitted Fergus. "And I did. But I worked something out."

"When you and Chimp went off?"

Fergus nodded.

"On your bike?" she added.

Fergus felt his heart leap like a highland salmon. "Shhhh!" he hushed. "How did you know?"

"I'm not daft," whispered Daisy. "I know you disappear off sometimes. I just wish I knew where. Don't worry, though, no one else has even an inkling."

"Thank goodness for that." Fergus breathed deeply, grateful that Daisy was so loyal, even if she did have eyes in the back of her head.

"So what *did* you work out?" she asked.

"Yes, do tell," said Wesley, who'd caught up, and was moodily pushing his own machine with Dermot.

"Okay," said Fergus. "If we're going to win the Internationals, we need to think outside the box – that's just like Charlie said. But more importantly we need to be hungry for it. I mean *really* hungry.

And not the cake kind." He frowned at Dermot who was busy demolishing a doughnut.

"And you think the Wreck-it Run will make that happen?" asked Mikey, sounding less than convinced.

Fergus stopped, and smiled. "Yes, I really do."

The others pulled up too and looked at the competition already lining up. There were all sorts of machines, and all sorts of people pushing and steering them, and most of them looked a lot more ready for the race than any of Hercules' Hopefuls, including Grandpa and Choppy themselves, who were still bickering, but clearly ready for action.

Charlie scooted up to them, smiling widely. "So, squad. Want to be back on your bikes?"

"Yup," said Minnie.

"Yu-huh," agreed Belinda.

"Like nothing else," said Wesley.

"There you go," said Charlie. "You're ready. Mission accomplished. Now all you need to do is smash the Wreck-it Run!"

Chimp barked in agreement and jumped up onto Charlie's lap.

Fergus smiled. This was going to be a disaster, he was sure of it. But he was sure of something else too –it was going to be totally worth it.

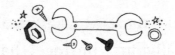

"Come on, Fergie!"

"Nice one, Dais!"

Fergus heard Jambo and Mum yelling from the crowds as he and Daisy sped round the second corner, Fergus braced low behind the push bars, Daisy with her knuckles white on the steering wheel.

He glanced to his left and then his right to see Wesley and Dermot on one side and Minnie and Belinda on the other. He daren't look behind, but up ahead wasn't looking too bad.

Calamity was crashing into all and sundry. Before hitting the buffers with Mikey, he'd taken out Grandpa and Choppy, but also the McTaggart brothers, Julie Gilhoolie the lollipop lady and her friend Selma, as well as Mr Minto the deputy head who was racing with the dinner lady Ms Grogan. That left Fergus and Daisy battling it out against the rest of the squad, and only one other crew up ahead. Fergus wasn't sure who they were, but they seemed pretty practised – more than him and Daisy, anyway.

"Come on," he called out to his co-driver.

"I am coming on!" she cried. "I'm steering for Scotland! You come on yourself!"

Fergus's legs were complaining, but he couldn't listen to them. Daisy was right, he had to dig deep for the last extra push.

Eyes on the prize, and on the crew standing between it and him, he dug deep, deep inside himself, searching for the courage it had taken Luke to get on that adapted bike, for the strength Scary Mary had shown to put her name down when she couldn't even speak it out loud, and, most of all, for the belief Charlie had had in all of them – that coming out of their comfort zone was the key to victory.

"Yee-hah!" yelled Daisy as they shot forward, leaving Dermot and Wesley, and Minnie and Belinda, struggling in their wake.

Fergus pounded the tarmac as the pram wheels spun. Grandpa and

Choppy's machine may have collapsed as soon as Calamity crashed into it, but the sledge was still secure. He and Daisy had a chance, if only they could catch up with that other crew.

If only . . .

Fergus ran and ran and ran, faster than when he had to run for the bus, faster than he'd ever managed to muster in athletics at school, faster even than the time he'd had to chase Mrs MacCafferty's cat, Carol, who was chasing Chimp. And they were making ground, metre by metre, so that, as they turned the final corner, they were almost neck and neck with the strangers.

But that's when it happened. There was a crack, and a crunch, and the steering wheel snapped off in Daisy's hands, sending the machine spinning into one of the safety hay bales, and sending Fergus flat on his face.

Lying on the floor, Fergus heard the cheer go up as the crowd congratulated the winners. But oddly, he didn't feel downhearted. In fact, all he felt was pure delight. They'd done it! So they'd been beaten at the final hurdle but it was a close-run thing, and they'd done themselves and Charlie proud, and that, he decided was all that mattered.

Fergus lifted himself up, dusted himself off, and, after rescuing Daisy from the hay and delivering her safely into Mrs Devlin's clasping arms, went to say a massive well done to the winners.

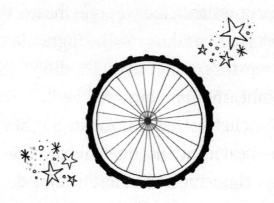

Three Cheers for Charlie

The week had been full of surprises, but there was one more in store for Fergus.

As the winners took off their helmets and grinned at the crowd, he saw the two girls were sisters, sharing the same green eyes and cheeky grin.

"That was quite a tumble," said the girl who'd been steering.

"Och, I'm fine," replied Fergus. "Or rather I will be," he added, feeling for the bruises he knew were on his knees, despite the padding.

"I'm Morgan and this is Sorcha," the girl said, and held out her hand.

"Fergus," he replied, shaking it, then turned to the other girl, shaking hers in turn. "You were brilliotic!" he added.

The girl touched the tips of her fingers to her chin and then towards Fergus.

"That means 'thanks'," Morgan explained.

She was deaf, Fergus realised quickly. He suddenly felt awful that he couldn't sign anything back.

The girl signed again.

Morgan grinned. "She says don't worry about it, you are an amateur after all. In signing as well as racing."

"An – an amateur?" Fergus stammered.

"Yes, aren't you?" asked Morgan. "We haven't seen you at the Wreck-it Run before."

"I'm . . . I'm a national champion," Fergus said. "Cycling, though," he added quickly.

The girls giggled and Fergus felt his pride, already pricked, deflate a little more.

"Och, we don't mean anything, do we, Sorcha?" said Morgan, signing as she spoke.

Sorcha shook her head.

"And we didn't mean to make assumptions. It's just this is our third year in a row in the Wreck-it Run, so we kind of know what we're doing. Whereas for you . . . well, this must have been –"

"Out of my comfort zone?" finished Fergus.

Sorcha signed at Fergus.

"Exactly that," translated Morgan, both her and her sister wearing warm smiles, which Fergus could tell were genuine.

Fergus smiled back. He liked these girls, and he knew he'd made some assumptions of his own lately, the whole squad had.

"You'd better get your prize," he said, as he saw Charlie waving frantically at them to hurry up.

Morgan followed his gaze. "Aye," she replied. "Come on, Sorcha."

Sorcha went to go, then, changing her mind, turned back to Fergus, nudging Morgan to watch her.

"I hope I'll see you again," Morgan said, as Sorcha signed the words. "Me too," she added.

"Me three," said Fergus. "Definitely."

As he lined up with the others to watch the pair being handed their gleaming trophy, and Jambo handing Mum the enormous cheque for the hospital from all the entrance money, Fergus felt himself soar inside – as if he'd just flown across a finish line on his very own bike.

"Three cheers for Charlie!" Fergus called out, as the squad assembled back at the track for the debrief. "Hip, hip . . ." He held his breath, hoping with all his heart that the rest of them felt the same as he did.

"Hooray!" came the reply. Not just once, or twice, but all three times, getting louder and louder with each.

"Thanks, squad," Charlie said when the hubbub had died down.

"No, thank *you*," said Fergus. "You were right all along. About the Wreck-it Run and the yoga."

"Well, maybe not yoga," whispered Wesley, who had still not quite mastered downward dog.

Charlie raised an eyebrow. "Ready to get back on your bikes, then?"

"Are you kidding?" Daisy cried.

"Now?" asked Belinda eagerly. "Can we? Can we?"

Charlie laughed. "Well, I reckon you're ready. But it's up to Herc and Choppy. They're your coaches, after all. My job here's done."

"Wait, you're leaving?" demanded Fergus.

"But – but –" stammered Calamity. "I thought . . ."

"Yeah, we thought that . . ." continued Minnie.

"You were on our side," Fergus finished. "That you'd stay with us until the Internationals." He'd not believed it possible when she first arrived, but now he really did want Charlie to stay. They all did! But instead she was quitting?

"Och, come on, sonny," Grandpa comforted. "Charlie *is* on your side. Always will be."

"I am," Charlie said. "And I'll be there on the big day cheering you on, but I've got my own team to think about, with a big tournament coming up. And, besides, I think you've learned just about all you can from me."

"No we haven't," Wesley pretended.

"I don't know what you're talking about," bluffed Belinda.

"Oh, I think you do," said Charlie.

"Fergus?" She turned to him, her smile wide, waiting.

He took a deep breath. "Never rest on your laurels," he said.

"Always think outside the box," added Daisy.

"Sometimes it's good to get out of your comfort zone," Mikey chipped in.

"Three out of three," Charlie said. "I knew you'd listened. Right, time for me to be off. So scoot, little fella," and she shooed Chimp out of her lap and back to Fergus's side, where he stayed for the walk back to the track, and the practice lap Choppy let them do as a reward, and all the way back to Napier Street and home.

"I'll not take anything for granted again," Fergus promised his dog as he slipped him a cold sausage he'd saved from his tea.

Chimp wolfed it down in one.

"It's . . . it's not just sausages you like me for though, is it?" Fergus asked.

Chimp licked his face.

Fergus smiled. "I guess that's my answer."

And Chimp licked and licked until all the ketchup was gone.

Joanna Nadin is an award-winning author of more than seventy books for children, including the bestselling Rachel Riley diaries, the Penny Dreadful series, and *Joe All Alone*, which is now being adapted for TV. She studied drama and politics at university in Hull and London, and has worked as a lifeguard, a newsreader and even a special adviser to the Prime Minister. She now teaches writing and lives in Bath, where she rides her rickety bicycle, but she never, ever back-pedals...

www.joannanadin.com

Clare Elsom is an illustrator of lots of lovely children's books, including the Furry Friends series, the Spies in Disguise series, the Maisie Mae series, and many more. She studied Illustration at Falmouth

University (lots of drawing) and Children's Literature at Roehampton University (lots of writing). Clare lives in Devon, where she can be found doodling, tap dancing and drinking cinnamon lattes.

www.elsomillustration.co.uk

Sir Chris Hoy MBE, won his first Olympic gold medal in Athens 2004. Four years later in Beijing he became the first Briton since 1908 to win three gold medals in a single Olympic Games. In 2012, Chris won two gold medals at his home Olympics in London, becoming Britain's most successful Olympian with six gold medals and one silver. Sir Chris also won eleven World titles and two Commonwealth Games gold medals. In December 2008, Chris was voted BBC Sports Personality of the Year, and he received a Knighthood in the 2009 New Year Honours List. Sir Chris retired as a professional competitive cyclist in early 2013; he still rides almost daily. He lives in Manchester with his family.

www.chrishoy.com

FLYING FERGUS

Trouble on the Track

It's decision time for Fergus and the rest of the squad. The Internationals are nearly here, and Hercules' Hopefuls need a starting line-up.

Tensions in the teams are riding high so the coaches decide to hold official trials: a timed knockout, a Keirin sprint and a road race.

With just four places at stake, who will be in . . . and who's out?

Catch up with Fergus and friends in their new adventure

COMING SOON